Guide smiley Sea Star to her best friend.

Start

W9-BZV-786

Finish

Around the Town

It's time for counting: 1, 2, 3.
Where could 5 bananas be?

Terrific Toys

Fruits and Vegetable.

Find the stickers to complete these objects.

square

semicircle

star

rectangle

triangle

circle

Daisy's Dresses

Kitty's Cakes

Can you find the stickers that complete each picture?

1 pineapple

2 robots

3 carrots

4 cupcakes

5 oranges

6 roses

7 dolls

8 tractors

9 pears

10 apples

Use the stickers to complete these animal faces.

Follow the lines to find out which pretty present belongs to which happy bunny.

In the Hotel

Tall and short, big and small.
Lots of opposites — find them all!

Restaurant

Reception

Can you find... over and under small and big

Kitchen

Find the stickers to complete these pictures of opposites.

BIG and SMALL

HOT

COLD

DAY

LOW and HIGH

NIGHT

Turn this **short** caterpillar into a **long** one!

Give this **slow** turtle a skateboard to make him **fast**.

choo choo!

Stick a train traveling **over** the bridge and a car **under** it.

beep beep!

On the Slopes

Sliding, jumping, falling down —
Find these actions, all around!

Let it snow!

Can you find... a bear waving   a fox throwing

Which skier left his lunchbox at the top of the mountain?

The mice have been building snowmen,
but only two are identical.
Can you find the snowman twins?

At the Park

BEEP and QUACK and TICK, TICK, TOCK —
Find the car and duck and clock!

Play area

tick!
tock!

boing!

zzz

quack!

Pond   Bandstand

Can you find...   a beeping car   a quacking duck

Can you find the sticker with the word that tells the sound each object makes?

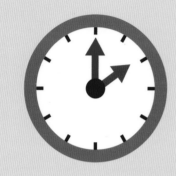 TICK TOCK!

 DING DONG!

 BOOM BOOM!

 TWEET TWEET!

 BEEP BEEP!

 CHOO CHOO!

 WOOF WOOF!

 MEOW MEOW!

Complete the sticker puzzle of the happy band!

What is your favorite instrument?

At the Train Station

Red and yellow, green and blue.
Let's find all these, and purple, too!

TICKETS

Yum
CHIPS
Yum

Take
the
train

Find the stickers to complete these pictures.

a green suitcase

a yellow book

a black cap

a pink cup

a gray teddy bear

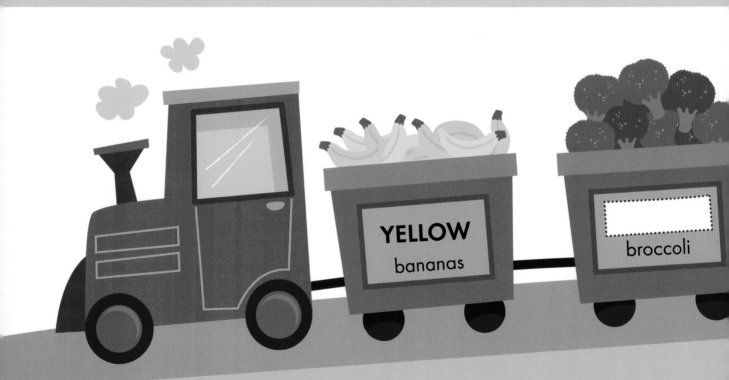

YELLOW
bananas

broccoli

a blue puddle

a purple shopping bag

a red hat

a brown chocolate bar

a white skirt

an orange cupcake

shells

balls

soil

This train is full of colorful things! Find the right word sticker to add to each train car. The first one is done for you.

At Preschool

Puzzle, paintbrush, book, and ball.
Hunt for words — let's find them all!

What things can you find to add to Frederick's school bag?

Frederick Fox

Trace the letters to spell these words.

apple   train

drum   house

At the Rec Center

What's in the scene that shouldn't be?
A dancing astronaut — can you see?

RECEPTION

11:00

Can you find the 10 differences between these pictures?

Who will dress as a scuba diver, and who will get dressed for dance class? Use the stickers to help these animals get ready!

At the Campground

Find the shorts and bathing suits.
See the coats and rubber boots!

All of these socks are in pairs... except for one!
Find and circle the sock that doesn't have a match.

Connect
the dots to
complete this
purr-fect shirt!

Answers

At the Beach

Start

Finish

At the Theme Park

On the Slopes

It's my lunchbox!

At the Park

 TICK TOCK!

 DING DONG!

 BOOM BOOM!

 TWEET TWEET!

 BEEP BEEP!

 CHOO CHOO!

 WOOF WOOF!

 MEOW MEOW!

At the Train Station

GREEN broccoli

BLUE shells

ORANGE balls

BROWN soil

At the Rec Center

At the Campground

I'm the odd sock!

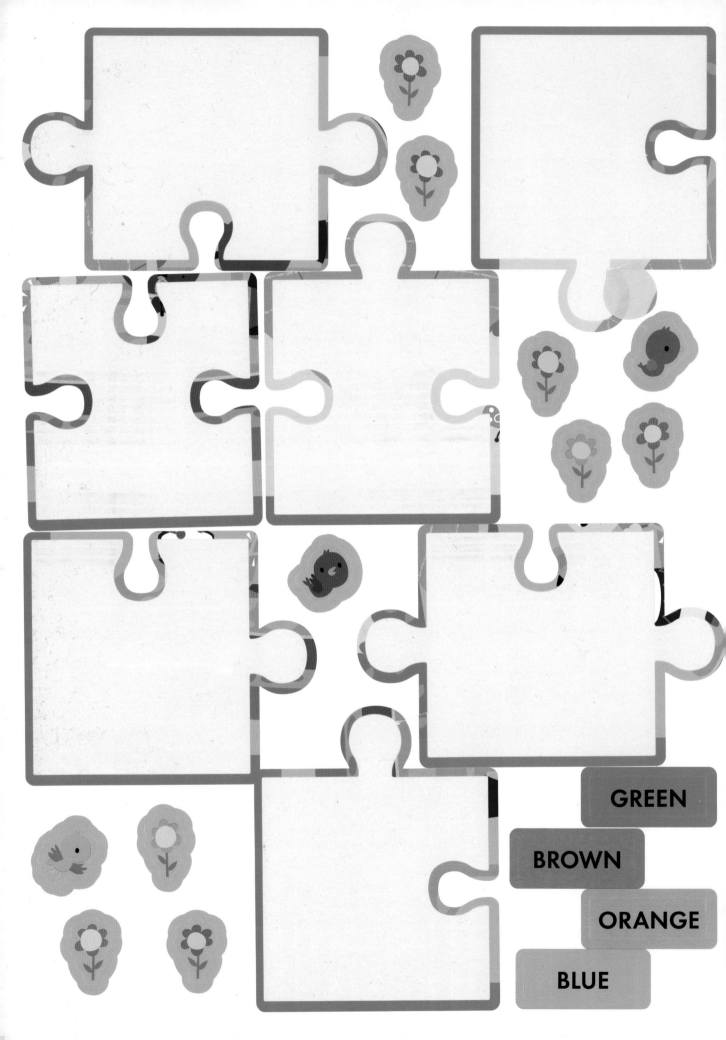

GREEN

BROWN

ORANGE

BLUE